one bear with bees in his hair

one bear with

For Vimbai and Binisa

Copyright © 1990 by Jakki Wood

All rights reserved.

CIP data is available.

First published in the United States 1991 by
Dutton Children's Books,
a division of Penguin Books USA Inc.

Originally published in 1990 by ABC
33 Museum Street, London WC1A 1LD

First American Edition   Printed in Hong Kong
10 9 8 7 6 5 4 3 2 1   ISBN 0-525-44695-8

bees in his hair

jakki wood

Dutton Children's Books   New York

One bear with bees in his hair.

Wait a minute—who goes there?

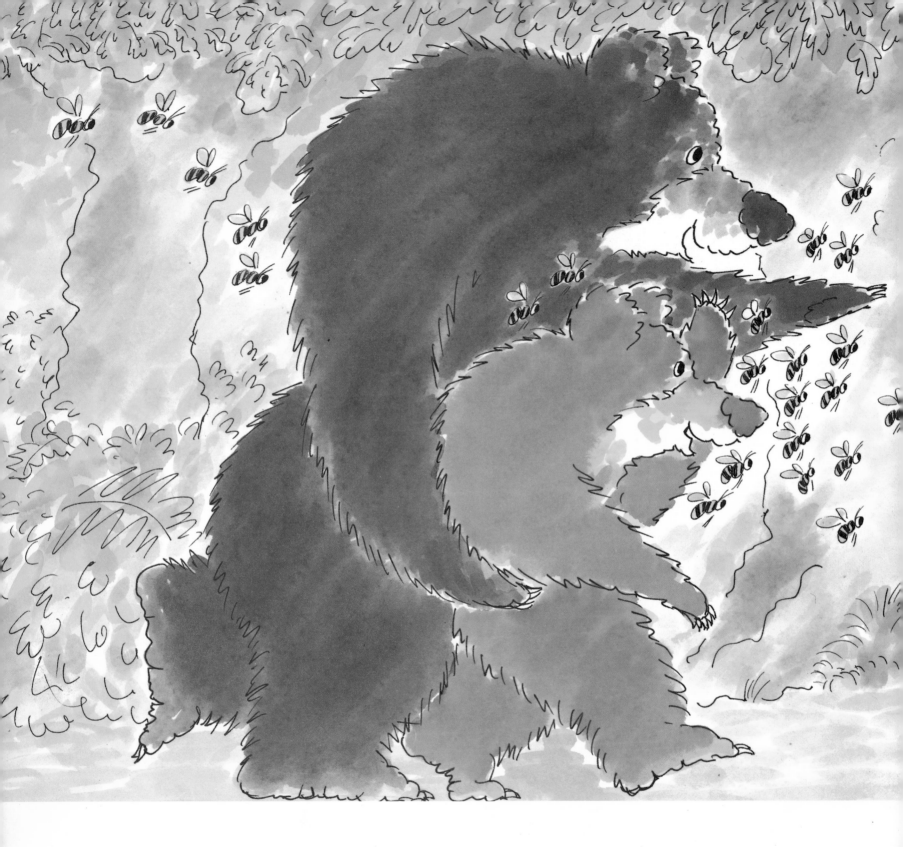

Two bears—that's more fun.

Oh, look! Another one.

Three hungry bears. But see . . .

Their bowls are empty. How can that be?

One bear more—that makes four.

Listen! Someone's at the door.

Open the door and see the sun.

All together, out bears run.

Five bears out of the house.

There's another, as still as a mouse.

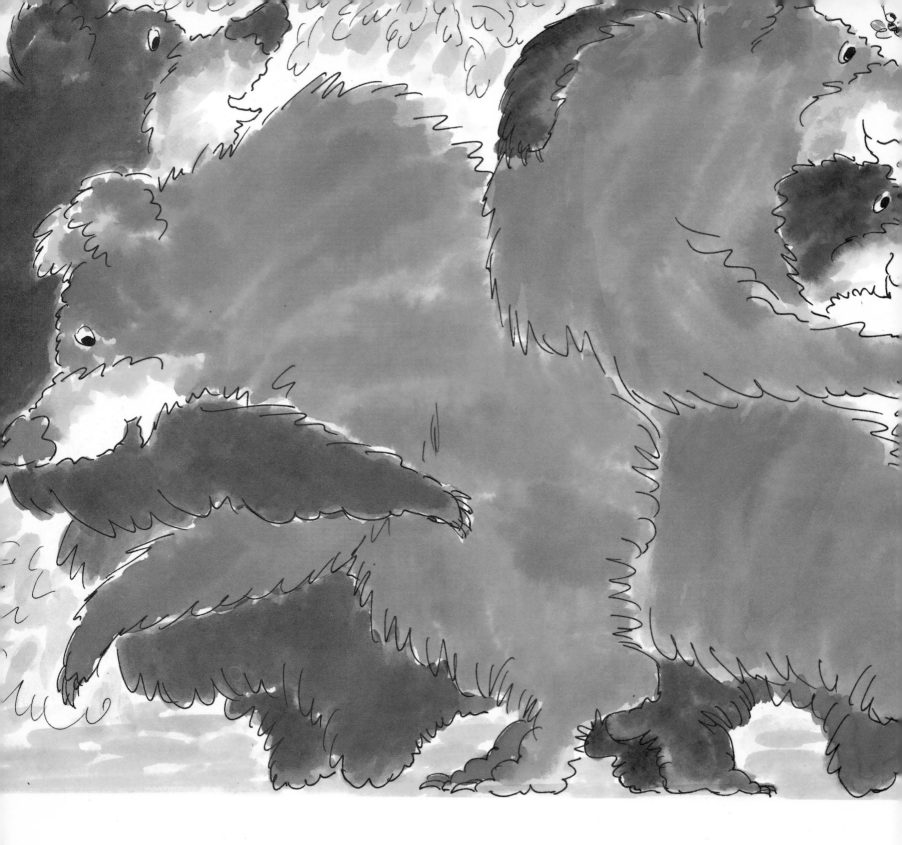

Six bears, waltzing along,

meet a big bear whistling a song.

Seven bears having a fling.

Here comes another. She likes to sing.

Eight bears having lots of fun.

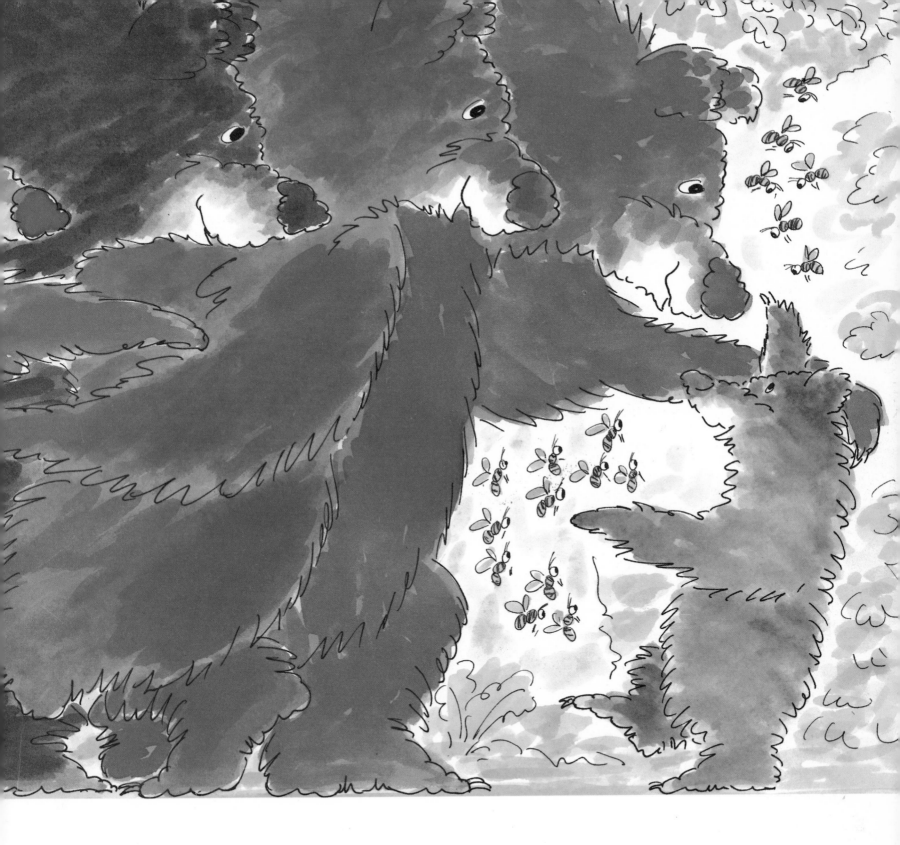

Come and join us, little one!

Nine bears playing hide-and-seek.

Close your eyes and don't you peek!

Ten bears now! For there's another,

near the tree with little brother.

That was fun—let's play again.

Close your eyes and count to ten.

Bears are hiding, near and far.

Can you see where all ten are?

One bear with bees in his hair.

Help him find the others . . . where?